This book is for

_____

With love from

_____

On this date

_____

BARN SANCTUARY®

THIS FARM IS A FAMILY

written by Dan McKernan

illustrated by Denise Hughes

ZONDERKIDZ

This Farm Is a Family
Copyright © 2022 by Dan McKernan and Barn Sanctuary

Requests for information
should be addressed to:

Zonderkidz, 3900 Sparks Dr. SE,
Grand Rapids, Michigan 49546

ISBN 978-0-310-74784-0 (hardcover)
ISBN 978-0-310-74813-7 (ebook)

Illustrated by: Denise Hughes
Art direction and design: Cindy Davis

Printed in Malaysia

It was a beautiful day at Barn Sanctuary, and the pasture, mud puddles, and pens were overflowing with happy animal sounds.

"COCK-A-DOODLE DOOOO!" crowed Roy the rooster.

DOOOOOO

MOOO

That woke Little Dude, who grunted and stretched, splashing mud onto Mike, who let out a loud MOOO! . . . which made Ginger stir and BAAA a morning greeting to Twitch . . . who did his silly little goat dance.

Just then, Mike heard something in the distance. "Farmer Dan is coming!" he shouted. Mike was blind and his horns were a bit lopsided, but his hearing was great. He loudly MOOOed again to greet his best bud.

Farmer Dan gave Mike a good chin scratch and
got a big wet pig smooch from Little Dude.

Farmer Dan loved all the animals at the sanctuary, from the pigs, turkeys, and donkeys to the ducks, chickens, sheep, and goats. They were all special, and together made one big happy family.

And this family gathered around Farmer Dan, waiting to hear his big news.

"We have a new cow coming today!" Farmer Dan announced. "Her name is Buttercup."

The chorus of excited moos, oinks, gobbles, quacks, baas, and brays that followed made Farmer Dan laugh.

"You guys are awesome! Okay, gang, I'm off! Lots to do to get ready for Buttercup!"

As Farmer Dan drove away, the animals all began talking at once.

Little Dude squealed, "Let's throw her a giant mud party!"

"Or how about an egg-citing egg hunt," Stanley the turkey suggested.

"I'm just happy to have a new friend to snuggle with!" said Ginger.

"Buttercup," Mike sighed. "She sounds so gentle and sweet! Do you think she likes tickles?"

But at a different farm on the other side of town, Buttercup wasn't thinking about parties or egg hunts, and certainly not snuggles or tickles.

She was in the middle of a temper tantrum. She snorted, kicked, and pawed the ground, especially if anyone tried to get close. Buttercup hadn't trusted anyone since her farmer died. Farmer Dan hoped she would feel better at the sanctuary.

But when he arrived to pick her up,
Buttercup did NOT want to get into the trailer . . .

. . . or in her new pen at Barn Sanctuary.

"Well, the mud party's out."

"Tickles would be too risky."

"I don't think she snuggles."

"That cow is mean!" shouted Steve the goat, who startled everyone.
Steve had a habit of appearing out of nowhere.

"I don't know," said Hugo the one-horned goat as he watched Buttercup anxiously pace. "Maybe she's just having a bad day. We should let her know we're friendly."

"WE MEAN NO HARM," Stanley said loudly.
"Seriously, Stanley?" Little Dude snorted. "She's not an alien!"
"Well, since a smile is a friend maker, let's all do that," Ginger said.

So the gang inched closer to Buttercup
and grinned from ear to ear.

The next day, the animals were back, determined to try again.

Stanley displayed his handsome feathers. Buttercup was not impressed.

Little Dude took her some hay, but Buttercup bellowed so loudly that it blew back the hairs on Little Dude's chin.

Hugo, Ginger, and Mike brought Buttercup gifts too, but that didn't end well.

The animals wondered, *was* Buttercup just a mean cow? They didn't really know.
But they did know for certain she didn't want them around. So, they decided to stay far away.

Then one day, Little Dude became curious and snuffled over to Buttercup's pen to sneak a peek at her. Where is that grouchy cow? he wondered.

"Buttercup's gone!" Little Dude shouted.
Everyone came running.
"Where did she go?" asked Ginger.
"I don't know, but we have to find her," said Mike.
"We do?" asked Stanley.
"Of course! She's prickly, but she's still part of the family!"
Mike gently reminded them.

The others agreed and
raced to find the missing cow.

Poor Buttercup was stuck. She didn't know whether to bellow or cry, scared she'd be stuck forever.

"Don't worry, Buttercup! We'll help you!" the animals all shouted.

They tried and they tried to unstick the poor cow, but nothing worked.

Suddenly Steve popped up out of nowhere, right under Buttercup's nose.

"What's up, Buttercup?"

The startled cow jumped and jerked and ended up twisting herself right out of the fence. She was free!

In their excitement, the animals surrounded Buttercup
and gave her a giant group hug.

"You've all been so sweet and kind," said Buttercup. "And I've just been angry and scared and . . . "

"Grumpy?" asked Steve.

"Yes, grumpy. So why did you help me?"

"Because that's what families do," Mike replied with a big smile. Then he heard a sound in the distance. "Here comes Farmer Dan!"

"So there's my new buddy!" Farmer Dan said as he walked up and gave Buttercup a neck scratch. "How about we all head over to the pasture and stretch our legs?"

A chorus of excited moos, oinks, gobbles, and baas told him that was an excellent idea.

So that's what they did.

And as they frolicked together in the green grass, Buttercup couldn't help but smile, knowing she had found a new family and her forever home.

Barn Sanctuary was established in 2016 in Chelsea, Michigan, in pursuit of a lofty mission to change the way the world views farmed animals by rescuing and rehabilitating abused and neglected farmed animals in need.

Barn Sanctuary provides a loving home specifically for farmed animals because they are historically the most mistreated group of animals in the world.

Barn Sanctuary is home to over 100 rescued farmed animals including cows, pigs, chickens, turkeys, ducks, sheep, and goats. Every rescue at Barn Sanctuary is treated as an individual deserving of empathy and respect.

We rely on donor support to do this life-saving work. If you would like to support one of our animals, please visit www.barnsanctuary.org/donate

Ginger

Buttercup

Little Dude

Mike

 BARN SANCTUARY®